D0013240

Robot on the Loose

ILLUSTRATED BY SCOTT GARRETT

Penguin Workshop
An Imprint of Penguin Random House

To children everywhere who are creative THINKERS & DOERS. And to Stacey always—HW

For my cherished daughters-in-law, Sarah and Julia. With love—LO

For all the brilliant art teachers out there enriching children's lives.—SG

PENGUIN WORKSHOP
Penguin Young Readers Group
An Imprint of Penguin Random House LLC

If you purchased this book without a cover, you should be aware that this book is stolen property. It was reported as "unsold and destroyed" to the publisher, and neither the author nor the publisher has received any payment for this "stripped book."

Penguin supports copyright. Copyright fuels creativity, encourages diverse voices, promotes free speech, and creates a vibrant culture. Thank you for buying an authorized edition of this book and for complying with copyright laws by not reproducing, scanning, or distributing any part of it in any form without permission. You are supporting writers and allowing Penguin to continue to publish books for every reader.

The publisher does not have any control over and does not assume any responsibility for author or third-party websites or their content.

Text copyright © 2018 by Henry Winkler and Lin Oliver Productions, Inc. Illustrations copyright © 2018 by Scott Garrett. All rights reserved. Published by Penguin Workshop, an imprint of Penguin Random House LLC, 345 Hudson Street, New York, New York 10014. PENGUIN and PENGUIN WORKSHOP are trademarks of Penguin Books Ltd, and the W colophon is a trademark of Penguin Random House LLC. Printed in the USA.

Typeset in Dyslexie Font B.V.
Dyslexie Font B.V. was designed by Christian Boer.

Library of Congress Cataloging-in-Publication Data is available.

ISBN 9780515157161 (pbk) 10 9 8 7 6 5 4 3 2 1
ISBN 9780515157178 (hc) 10 9 8 7 6 5 4 3 2 1

The books in the Here's Hank series are designed using the font Dyslexie. A Dutch graphic designer and dyslexic, Christian Boer, developed the font specifically for dyslexic readers. It's designed to make letters more distinct from one another and to keep them tied down, so to speak, so that the readers are less likely to flip them in their minds. The letters in the font are also spaced wide apart to make reading them easier.

Dyslexie has characteristics that make it easier for people with dyslexia to distinguish (and not jumble, invert, or flip) individual letters, such as: heavier bottoms (b, d), larger than normal openings (c, e), and longer ascenders and descenders (f, h, p).

This fun-looking font will help all kids—not just those who are dyslexic—read faster, more easily, and with fewer errors. If you want to know more about the Dyslexie font, please visit the site www.dyslexiefont.com.

CHAPTER 1

"Attention, all students," the voice on the school loudspeaker boomed. It was Principal Love. "We have just cleaned out the Lost and Found, and discovered thirty-seven single shoes," he announced. "A lot of you must be hopping home. If you are missing a shoe, please hop to Mrs. Crock's desk in the front office."

I looked down at my feet. I'm the kind of kid who would lose a shoe, but this time it wasn't me.

I'm proud to report that I had two matching blue shoes. Of course, my socks didn't match. One was yellow and one had stripes. I can only get so many things right at one time.

"We also found half a pickle," Principal Love went on. "But the owner does not have to come and pick that up."

"Hey, Zip," my best friend Frankie Townsend said with a laugh. "I bet that's yours."

Frankie has known me since we were babies. Anyone who's been

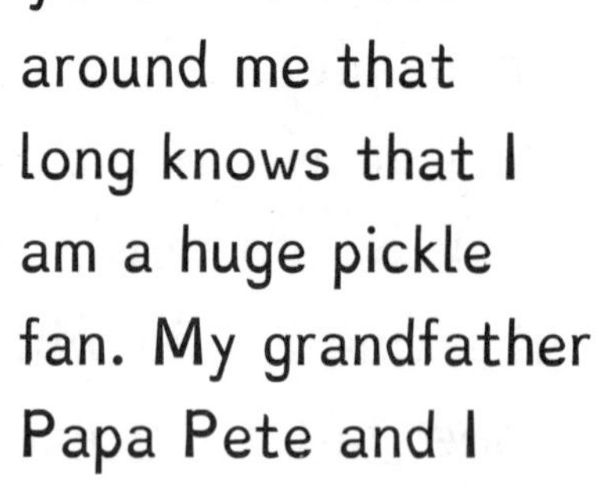

around me that long knows that I am a huge pickle fan. My grandfather Papa Pete and I always share a pickle when we have something serious to talk over. He says pickles clear the brain.

The recess bell rang, and we all got up and headed for the door. But then we realized that Principal Love had more to say. I should have known. He *always* has more to say.

"Let me remind you that Friday is our Build-a-Robot competition," he announced. "This year, the competition is open to our second- and third-graders. We have made a special category for beginning builders. You can power your robots simply with a motor and a remote control. No need for computer skills. Isn't that exciting?"

"It'd be more exciting if he said

we could have the rest of the week off school," I muttered.

"I'm looking forward to seeing all of your dazzling creations," Principal Love went on. "Until then, this is your principal and my pet frog, Fred, saying 'ribbit.' That is all."

My other best friend, Ashley Wong, cracked up. She thinks it's so funny that Principal Love is always putting Fred on the loudspeaker. Principal Love thinks that just because he understands frog talk, the rest of us do, too.

Ashley, Frankie, and I *ribbitt*ed all the way down the hall.

"I'm going to enter the Build-a-Robot contest," I said as we walked down the stairs.

"You can't just enter," Ashley said. "You have to sign up on the bulletin board outside Principal Love's office."

"Okay, I'll do it after recess," I said.

"You better do it right now," Frankie answered. "I know you. And you know you. 'I forgot' is your middle name."

We stopped outside Principal Love's office door. There was a bulletin board with a pencil on a string. I took the pencil and proudly wrote "**HANK ZIPZER**" on line 10.

"It's official," I said to Frankie

and Ashley. "I can hardly wait. I have some great robot ideas sitting right here in my mind, in between my phone number and last week's spelling words. All I have to do is build my little robot."

"Hank, you're not being realistic," Ashley said. "That robot contest was announced a month ago. All the other kids have been building their robots for weeks."

"So?" I said. "I'll work fast. I'll just give it the old Zipzer attitude."

"Hank," Frankie said. "The contest is on Friday. As in the day after tomorrow."

"So I'll work *extra* fast."

"You can't build a whole robot

in a day," Ashley pointed out.

"Oh yeah? Just watch me. I'm going to start collecting robot parts right now."

We walked out onto the playground. I looked around at the swings and slides and handball court and sandbox and benches. I didn't see one thing that looked like a robot to me. What I did see was a kid I had never noticed before. He was sitting by himself on a bench along a fence. He looked like any other third-grader except he was wearing a tie and a vest, which was all buttoned up. The reason I noticed him, aside from his weird clothes, was that he was building a robot.

The robot had four silver rods for legs and a long tail that swayed back and forth. The kid was taking something that looked like a head out of a shoebox. We stood and watched him for a minute as he attached the head to the body with the smallest screwdriver I had ever seen.

"Wow," I said to Frankie and Ashley. "That guy seems like a robot expert. Let's go see what he's doing. I bet he'll give me some tips."

We walked up to him, and I introduced myself.

"Hi," I said. "I'm Hank Zipzer, and these are my best friends, Frankie and Ashley."

I waited for him to say hi, but he didn't even look up. He just kept turning the screwdriver like we weren't even there.

"That's a really cool robot," I went on.

Nothing. No answer. I looked at Frankie and Ashley, and they shrugged.

"I'm entering the robot contest, too," I said.

"Jaden," he said suddenly.

"Excuse me?"

"I'm Jaden."

"Oh, nice to meet you, Jaden," I said. "I just came over to see if

you had any tips on robot building."
There was a long silence while he continued to focus only on his robot. None of us knew what to say. So I said the first thing that came to my mind.

"Your robot looks like a dragon," I said. "Does it breathe fire?"

Jaden stopped what he was doing and looked up at me for one second.

"Dog," he said.

"It breathes dogs?" I answered. "That's weird."

"Maybe it breathes mini dogs," Frankie said.

"Yeah, like little hot dogs," Ashley added. "If you're hungry, you push a button and it spits out a mini hot dog."

We all cracked up, except for Jaden. I wondered why he wasn't laughing. I mean, let's face it, a robot spitting out mini hot dogs is funny. But not to Jaden. He just reached into the shoe box and pulled out another screw.

"Okay," I said to him. "Obviously talking is not your favorite thing, so we'll be going."

Just as we turned to leave, Jaden started to talk.

"Specifically," he blurted out, "this robot is an Alaskan husky. I am wiring it to bury bones, which is a behavior that many huskies use to protect their food."

"Hey, that's more like it," I said.

Maybe this kid was more talkative than I had thought.

"Listen," I said. "I know I'm a little late getting started, but I'm going to build my robot tonight. I could really use any tips you can give me."

"You need to begin with a blueprint that has all your technical data," he said. "You'll need a protractor, a sharp pencil, and all your math skills. When you begin the building stage, of course, you'll need the proper number of wires plus your robot's body parts. Then simply choose the right motor, the correct size batteries, and your remote control method. That's all there is to it."

My brain walked away before my body did.

"Okay," I said. "Thanks so much. That was really helpful."

As we walked away, Frankie looked at me and said, "Exactly how much of that did you understand?"

"Exactly zero," I answered.

"So you've decided not to enter the robot contest," Ashley said. "I think that's a good idea. You can try out for the school play instead."

"No, I'm not quitting," I said. "I'm just going to do it my way."

"And what way is that?" Frankie asked.

That was a good question, and I had no answer.

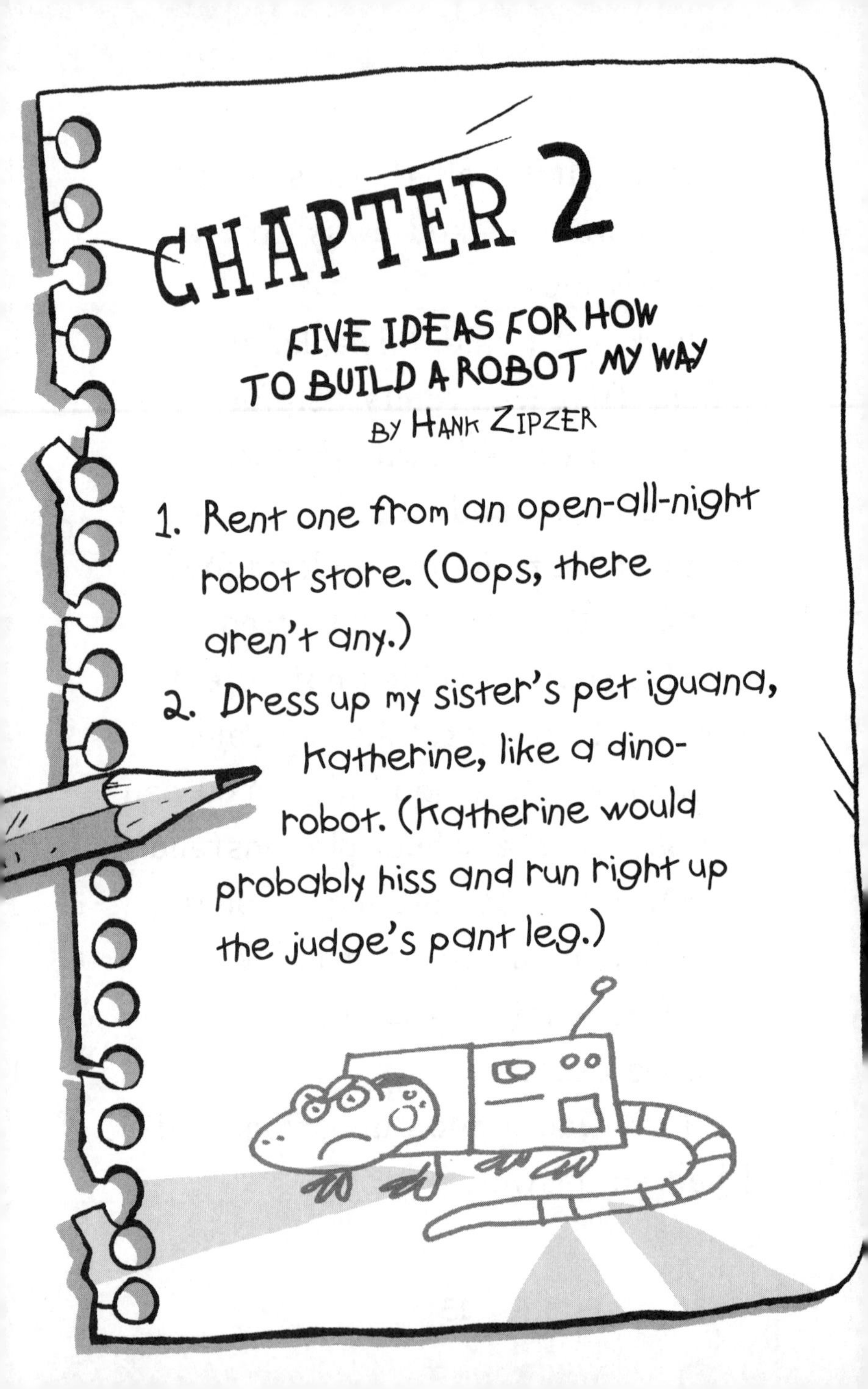
CHAPTER 2
FIVE IDEAS FOR HOW TO BUILD A ROBOT MY WAY
BY HANK ZIPZER
1. Rent one from an open-all-night robot store. (Oops, there aren't any.)
2. Dress up my sister's pet iguana, Katherine, like a dino-robot. (Katherine would probably hiss and run right up the judge's pant leg.)

3. Dress up my sister, Emily, like a robot. (Actually, I wouldn't have to do a lot of dressing.)

4. Forget I ever said anything about entering the contest. (Nope, I said I was going to build a robot, and I will.)

5. I don't have time for Number 5. I have to go build a robot.

NOTES
DA

CHAPTER 3

Frankie, Ashley, and I all gathered around my dining-room table after school that day.

"Welcome, everyone, to the first official planning meeting for how to build my robot," I said, making my voice sound big and serious.

"Hank, why are you making an announcement?" Frankie asked. "It's only us."

"I wanted to remind everyone why we're here."

"We remember why we're here," Ashley said.

"Actually, I was reminding myself. I forget things very easily. So, the meeting will now begin. What do we do next?"

Frankie raised his hand.

"Yes, Frankie," I said, calling on him.

"How about if you get started?" he suggested. "Ashley and I are here to help you."

"Excellent idea." I waited for a minute, then said, "I just wish I knew how to do that."

"I think you need to make a blueprint," Ashley said, "like that kid Jaden said."

That was also a good idea,

except none of us knew what a blueprint was.

Just then, my dad came in from the kitchen, carrying a plate of celery sticks stuffed with cream cheese.

"I made a snack for you kids," he said, grabbing a couple of sticks for himself.

"Thanks, Dad," I said. "By the way, do you happen to know what a blueprint is?"

"Certainly," he answered. "It's a drawing you make before building something. It gives you a plan to follow."

"Why didn't Jaden just say that we had to make a drawing?" I wondered. "What's with the blueprint thing?"

"He always uses big words," Frankie said. "My brother's in his third-grade class and says nobody can understand him when he talks. Mostly he hangs out by himself and doesn't have any friends."

"He must be so lonely," Ashley said.

"Well, then maybe he should try using shorter words so people can understand him," I said. "Anyway, all this talk about Jaden isn't helping me make a blueprint."

"If you're going to make one, you'll need paper, a ruler, colored pencils, and a protractor," my dad pointed out.

"I have no idea what a protractor is, Dad, except the word is fun to say."

"It's like a ruler used to measure angles," he explained. "It's shaped like a half moon."

"Oh, that thing on my desk! I've been using it as a back scratcher."

Frankie cracked up. "Well, how about getting all that stuff from your room," he suggested.

"Let me go get the supplies," my dad said. "If Hank goes to

look for them, we might never see him again." He turned to me. "Remember yesterday when you went to change your shirt before dinner? You got lost reorganizing your desk drawer, and we had to come get you."

"Hey, I can't help it if I like to keep my desk drawer neat," I said.

"Neat!" my dad said. "There's nothing neat about your room. Some of the dirty socks lying around your room have been there since you were three."

Frankie laughed loudly. I had to admit that was funny.

"My room looks like that, too," he said. "There's a pile of socks in the corner so high, my mom calls it Sock Mountain."

"Picking up socks and throwing them in the hamper is so annoying," Ashley said. "My room looks like it snowed socks."

"Guys," I said. "Listen to what we're saying. There's the robot idea. I'm going to build a sock-picker-upper robot. This is going to change the lives of kids all over the country."

"I got to hand it to you, Hankster," Frankie said. "That is one great idea."

"You could sell them, you know," Ashley chirped, pushing her glasses up on her nose. "Every kid is going to want one. Frankie and I will help you sell them. We'll start with our school, then the city. I can already see the billboard in Times Square!"

"Whoa there, kids," my dad said. "Just build the first one. Then you can think about billboards."

My dad went into my room to get the supplies. While he was gone, Ashley, Frankie, and I talked nonstop about my robot, which had suddenly become *our* robot. They were as excited as I was.

"It has to have big claws to pick up the socks," Frankie said.

"And long arms so it can reach under the bed," Ashley added.

"And a nose clip like the ones swimmers use so it doesn't pass out from the stinky socks," I concluded.

It was really exciting to have so many ideas coming all at once. When my dad came back in with the pencils, ruler, protractor, and a big piece of white construction paper, we were ready to draw a blueprint.

"There you go," he said. "Don't make it too complicated, because remember, you have to build this thing and you don't have much time."

We took our places on either side of the table, but when we tried to put the paper in the middle, there wasn't enough room. My dad's computer, notebooks, and mechanical pencils took up most of the table.

"No offense, Dad," I said, "but your work stuff is kind of in our way."

"Hank, can I just point out that you're in *my* work place?"

"How about if today your work place is the kitchen table," I suggested. "Wouldn't that be fun? You could type on your computer with one hand and open the refrigerator with the other. I happen to know there are some of your favorite ice-cream sandwiches in the freezer."

"Okay, Hank," my dad said. "I know you're in a time crunch, so I'll let you kids work here. I'll move my stuff into the kitchen."

"Thanks, Dad."

After he left, we each picked up a pencil. Mine was green because it's my favorite color. We all just sat there staring at the paper. No one drew even a line.

"We can't really design this robot if it doesn't have a name," Ashley said.

"So what we need is the name of a great sock-picker-upper," Frankie said. "We could name it after my grandmother, Rosalee. She was great at picking up socks with her cane and flicking them into the hamper."

From the kitchen, I could hear the freezer door opening. My dad was already into the ice-cream sandwiches. That gave me an idea.

"How about Stanley, after my dad," I said. "As far as sock-picker-uppers go, he's right up there with the best of them. And besides, he did give us his work space."

"Hmm," Ashley said. "Stanley the Robot. I like it."

"Sounds good to me," Frankie agreed.

"Sounds good to me, too," my dad shouted from the kitchen.

We all high-fived. Stanley it was.

Our robot had a name. All he needed now was legs, arms, a head, a motor, and a body.

In other words, everything!

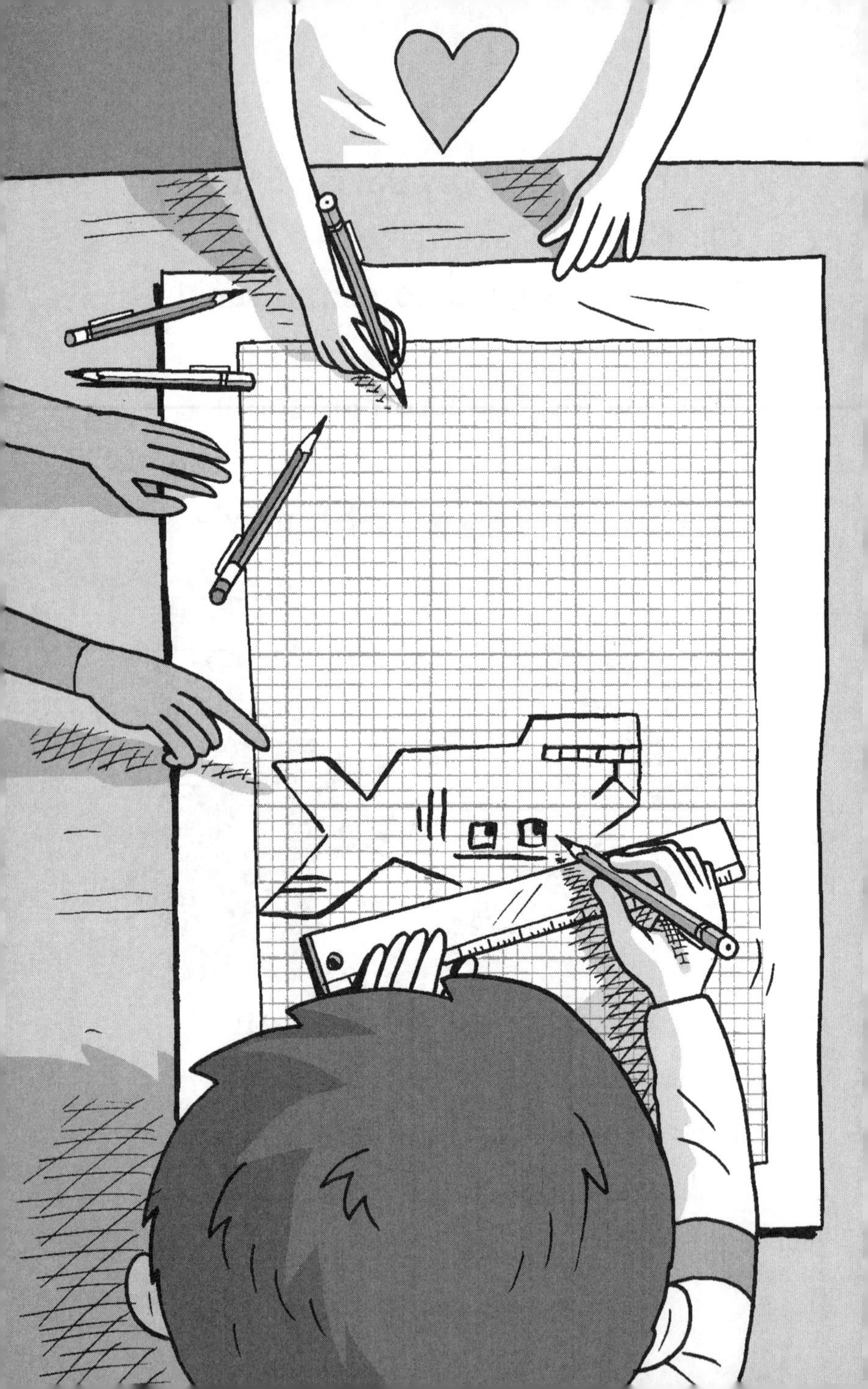

CHAPTER 4

We had been working on our blueprint for almost an hour and had finally finished something that looked like a face. Well, it didn't look like a human face—more like a combination of a fish and a kangaroo, if you can imagine that.

"Stanley's kind of ugly," Frankie commented.

"But in an adorable kind of way," Ashley said.

When we started to design the body, poor Stanley got even

weirder. He had a long chest, and wheels for legs. The wheels turned out to be square because I used the ruler to draw them. I didn't think about the fact that rulers only go in straight lines, not in circles. Sometimes I don't plan ahead. My dad always says, "If you fail to plan, then you are planning to fail." He says that almost every night when it's bedtime and I still haven't finished my homework.

Frankie and Ashley didn't mind the square wheels.

"We know what you meant," Frankie said. "Everybody knows

that in real life, wheels are round."

Of course that's exactly when my know-it-all sister, Emily, walked into the dining room and shot a glance at our robot design.

"I bet Hank drew those square wheels," she said. "He doesn't even know what a wheel is."

"At least I don't have a scaly iguana with a mile-long tongue riding around on my shoulder," I shot back.

Katherine looked me right in the eye and hissed. Then her little legs pushed off Emily's shirt, and she flew through the air, landing smack on top of our blueprint.

"Hey, Emily," Frankie said. "Tell your lizard to move. We're doing serious work here. We've got a sock-picker-upper robot to build."

"Katherine is very curious," Emily said. "I'm sure she just wants to get a good look at your robot plans."

"Are you saying your lizard can read?" Ashley asked.

"Who are we to know?" Emily said. "They're very intelligent creatures."

"Well, your intelligent creature just pooped a pile of green stuff all over Stanley," I said.

Emily broke into a big smile and reached out to pick up Katherine.

"Good girl," she said. "You remembered to use the paper." Turning to us, she added, "I told you she is very intelligent."

"Well, so much for our blueprint," I said. "I'm not getting anywhere near it now."

"That's okay," Ashley said. "We all know what we have to do to build Stanley. Let's go find the parts."

"We can start in the kitchen," I said. "There's lots of cool stuff there."

As we got up from the table, Emily started to follow us.

"Sorry," I said to her. "This is

for humans only. So I guess that leaves both Katherine *and* you out."

"Fine," Emily said. "We have better things to do, anyway. Katherine and I are going to the bathroom for our afternoon toothbrushing session."

"Great. Maybe you can potty train her while you're there."

"Maybe I will," Emily said. "Then she'll be ahead of you."

That did it. We left and went into the kitchen. My dad was sitting at the table, with two ice-cream sandwich wrappers next to his computer.

"How are the plans coming?" he asked.

"Katherine had an accident on

them," Frankie explained. "So we're moving right into the next stage: building Stanley."

My dad raised his eyebrows and chuckled. "It's nice that you named your robot after me."

A big smile broke out across his face. I wondered if this was a good time to ask him if we could move my bedtime a half hour later. But there wasn't time, because Frankie and Ashley already had all the kitchen drawers open.

"I think we should use spoons for Stanley's arms," Frankie said.

"Yes," Ashley agreed. "Spoons will be good for picking up socks."

"Don't use our good silverware," Dad said. "Your mother will be very upset if two spoons are missing."

I searched around in the drawer, and at the very back found a baby spoon with a pink polka-dot handle in the shape of a kitten.

"I remember this," I said. "It was Emily's kitty cat spoon. She couldn't say spoon, so she called it her *'oon*. That was when she was still cute."

"Let's use it," Ashley said. "We want Stanley to be colorful and cute."

"Well, he won't be so cute if he only has one arm," Frankie said.

"And it looks like you Zipzers are out of baby spoons."

I opened the drawer my mom calls the "one of everything drawer." It's where she puts stuff that doesn't have a place anywhere else. There's one battery, one hammer, one chopstick, one rubber band, and one instruction book on how to use the icemaker. Luckily, there was also a baggie filled with plastic forks that came with our takeout Chinese food.

"Bingo," Frankie said. "We now have Stanley's other arm. One of these forks can hold the sock in place while the spoon scoops it up."

"But, Hank, don't you think Stanley's arms should match?" Ashley said.

"Not my robot," I said. "Stanley's one of a kind."

I could hear my dad chuckle from the kitchen table.

"You bet I am, kids," he said, grinning. "Spread it around the neighborhood."

"I hope this plastic fork is strong enough to hold a sock," Frankie said.

"Let's test it out," I suggested. I plopped down on the floor and took off my sneakers and socks.

"Whoa," Frankie said, holding his nose. "You got some major foot smell going on there, Zip."

"I guess I should have taken a pair of clean socks out of the drawer this morning," I said, "instead of picking these up from under the bed."

"We can't let smell get in the way of science," Ashley said.

She got a pair of salad tongs out of the drawer. I looked over at my dad, and he was concentrating really hard on his computer screen. Ashley covered her nose with her hand. Then she bent down, picked up one sock, and flicked it across the kitchen floor.

Frankie held the spoon, and I held the plastic fork. Together, we crawled toward the sock as if we were Stanley. Frankie slid the spoon under the sock and scooped it up. It held the sock perfectly.

"Spoon all clear for duty," he reported.

Then he flicked the sock over to me. I speared it with the plastic fork and lifted my arm up, making a robot sound.

"Stanley . . . happy . . . ," I said. "Stanley . . . pick . . . up . . . sock."

"Stanley hold nose," Frankie said.

It was working. Using both the spoon and the fork, Stanley had picked up his first sock.

"We did it, guys," I said. "Thanks to you, I'm on the way to winning this competition. Now let's take a snack break. I happen to know the location of three fun-size bags of BBQ potato chips."

"Are you kidding?" Frankie said. "There's a ton of work left to do."

"Stanley only has arms,"

Ashley said. "He still needs a body, wheels, and a motor."

"And a face," I said. "I think he should look like a combination of a garbage truck and a triceratops."

"You won't find a face like that under a couch pillow," Frankie said. "We have to start building."

"Do you think you'll be able to finish in time?" Ashley asked.

My brain told me the answer was no. But my Zipzer attitude wasn't going to let me give up.

"Forget the BBQ chips," I said. "Come on, guys. We have a robot to build!"

FACTS
IGUAN
LEGO

CHAPTER 5

Frankie and Ashley went into my room to look for parts for Stanley's body. I went into Emily's room to see what I could find. I found a box of princess Legos that someone had given her for her birthday. She had never even opened the box. Emily is not the kind of person who wants to build a pink princess castle. Now, if it had been a lizard Lego kit, she would have built it in two seconds.

"What do you think you're doing?" a voice from behind me said.

I'm sure you already guessed that it was Emily's voice. Even though she and Katherine had returned from the bathroom, Katherine's teeth seemed as yellow as ever.

"I really need this box of Legos to build my robot," I begged.

"They belong to me."

"I know, but you've never even taken the ribbon off. Come on, Emily. You're not ever going to use these Legos."

"What are you going to give me for them?"

"I'm giving you the wonderful feeling of getting to help your older brother."

"Three nights of you doing the dishes," she fired back. "That's the deal."

Normally, I would not have made that deal, but I was running out of time.

"Fine," I said, tucking the Lego box under my arm and bolting for the living room.

Frankie and Ashley were waiting for me with a pile of things they had gathered.

"We got some cool stuff," Frankie said. "Look, here's some

pencils and rubber bands."

"What are those for?" I asked. "Stanley's not going to write anything."

"The pencils are going to make his arms longer," Ashley said. "If they aren't long enough, he won't be able to scoop up the socks."

"And look at this," Frankie went on. "We also took the remote control and a motor from your old yellow front loader truck. I hope you don't mind if it never runs again."

"That's okay," I said. "Cheerio chewed off the digging bucket, anyway. What good is a front loader without a bucket? It's like hot chocolate without the chocolate."

"We also took two wheels off your old monster truck," Ashley said.

"How come only two? Stanley needs four wheels."

"The front wheels were missing in action," Frankie said. "But we could get the other two wheels off your cement mixer."

"I love that truck," I said. "Every time I got sick and stayed home from school, Mr. Cement Mixer always made me feel better.

I can't take him apart, not even for Stanley."

"Well, we need to find something that's round and rolls," Ashley said. "Anyone have a bright idea?"

"Golf balls?" Frankie suggested.

I shook my head. "We don't have any. My dad says golf gives him a rash. I never asked him where."

"Some parent things you just don't want to know," Frankie said with a nod.

"How about pizza cutters?" Ashley said. "They're round."

"Too sharp," I answered. "Besides, we only have one of them."

"Think, guys," Ashley said. "What's round and rolls?"

"Meatballs," Frankie said. "A Frisbee. Marbles. Doughnuts. A sandwich roll."

"Or toilet paper rolls," I said, joining in the list.

"Are those strong enough to hold Stanley?" Ashley asked.

"Legos aren't that heavy," I answered. "And besides, we only need Stanley to work for a few minutes. It's not like he's got to roll all the way across the Brooklyn Bridge."

"Let's try it," Frankie said. "It's the best idea we have."

We all jumped up and raced to the bathroom.

"What we need is the cardboard tube inside the roll of toilet paper," I said. "We'll cut it in two pieces, wrap the pieces in Scotch tape to make them stronger, and presto, Stanley will have himself two front wheels. Okay, team. Let's start unrolling."

"Wait a minute," Ashley said. "What are we going to do with all the toilet paper we take off the roll? We can't waste it. Some poor tree gave its life for this."

"How about if we tear it into little squares and pile it up on the back of the toilet?" Frankie asked.

"Great idea," I said. "Frankie and I will make the squares, and Ashley, you make a sign that says: *Attention, all Zipzers, get your toilet paper here.* I'd do it, but I don't know how to spell *toilet*. Or *attention*."

When we were finished, we took the cardboard toilet paper tube back into the living room, cut it in two even pieces, and wound a lot of Scotch tape around them.

If you closed your eyes, you'd have thought they were wheels. Sort of. Then we sat down in a circle.

"Okay," I said. "Project Build a Robot, Part 2, is officially starting. Ready, set, go!"

We began with the pink Legos. Using a big flat piece of the castle floor as the platform for Stanley's body, we built up his stomach and chest with lots of square blocks. Then we attached his spoon and fork arms. It was amazing to see Stanley take shape right in front of our very eyes. Too bad he was still missing a head.

"We could use a head from one of the Lego people," Ashley suggested. "This set comes with a princess, a knight, and some unicorns. I vote for the unicorn."

"You don't think Stanley will be embarrassed having a sparkly horn coming out of his head?" I asked.

"Embarrassed?" Ashley exclaimed. "Of course not. Don't you know that unicorns are the symbol of success?"

"In that case," I said, "let's give him two horns. Or maybe even three."

Frankie dug through all the Lego pieces and came up with two unicorn heads.

"Okay," I said. "Let's tape them

on. One thing is for sure. No one else in the contest is going to have a two-headed unicorn sock-picker-upper robot."

Now that Stanley had heads, he needed wheels. Putting wheels under his platform was a little bit hard. We had to attach the monster truck wheels to the ends of a pencil, and tape the pencil onto the back of his platform. Then we did the same with the toilet roll wheels. We taped them and their pencil to the front of Stanley's platform. That gave him wheels to roll on.

From the waist down, Stanley looked like a very weird steamroller. From the waist up, he looked like a crazy two-headed, two-horned unicorn. But I wasn't going to tell him.

"Now we have to attach the motor," I said.

"And figure out how it's going to make the wheels turn and the arms lift," Frankie added quickly.

"That sounds like it's going to take a while," Ashley said, pushing her glasses up on her nose.

"Wait a minute," Frankie said. "Anyone know what time it is? I have to be home for dinner at five thirty. Tonight's my night to set the table."

We checked the clock, and the news wasn't good. It was almost five thirty.

"We better hurry," Ashley said. "Because I have to be home for dinner, too."

I picked up the motor and the remote control and just stared at them as if they were aliens from another planet.

"What are you waiting for, Zip?" Frankie asked.

"I don't have a clue what to do with this motor."

"Neither do I," Ashley said.

"Me either," Frankie said.

There was a lot of silence. Suddenly, it seemed like Project Stanley was doomed. What good is a robot that can't move?

CHAPTER 6

Frankie and Ashley and I decided that our best chance to make Stanley come alive was to see if Jaden would help me. He seemed to know everything about robots that I didn't. Before Frankie and Ashley left my apartment, we decided to try to find Jaden at recess the next day and ask his advice.

In the morning, I packed Stanley in one of my mom's recycled grocery bags. It smelled a little like hamburger meat, but Stanley never mentioned that he was a vegetarian, so I didn't think he would mind. Of course, if I had been in there, all I'd be thinking about was a cheeseburger with extra ketchup and pickles.

I put Stanley's motor and the remote control in a nest of some of the leftover toilet paper, to protect them from bouncing around on the walk to school. Ashley was very proud that the paper didn't go to waste.

We asked my dad to walk us to school early so we could hang out on the playground and see if Jaden showed up.

"I think you should use the extra time to study for your

spelling test," my dad said as he dropped us off at the front door. Principal Love, who greets all of us at the entrance every morning, overheard what my dad said.

"Ah yes," he said. "Spelling. Nothing thrills me like a word spelled correctly. Take *receive*, for instance."

"I'd rather not," I mumbled.

"R-E-C-E-I-V-E," Principal Love said. "That's music to my ears."

"Not to mine," I said. "It's just a bunch of letters that I can never get in the right order."

We scooted out of there before Principal Love could go on about the wonders of spelling.

"Let's see if Jaden is on that same bench where he was yesterday," Frankie said.

We hurried to the bench by the fence, but Jaden wasn't there.

We looked around the lunch tables, the handball court, and even peeked into the attendance office. The only person there was Mrs. Crock, eating a drippy egg sandwich.

"Can I help you, kids?" she asked, with what looked like an entire loaf of bread wedged between her teeth.

"We're looking for Jaden," Ashley said.

"Would that be Jaden S. or Jaden W.?"

"The Jaden who has trouble talking," I said. "Not that there's anything wrong with that."

"Oh, that would be Jaden W."

"I really need his help," I said.

"His mom called and said he'll be

late today," Mrs. Crock said. "Why don't you look for him at lunch?"

We went to class, and I put the bag with Stanley underneath my desk. It wasn't long before I felt Nick McKelty's stinky breath on the back of my neck. He leaned his soccer-ball-size head over my shoulder to peek inside the bag.

"What's in there, Zipperbutt?" he asked. "You're playing with your teeny tiny unicorn Legos again? I haven't done that since kindergarten."

Leave it to McKelty to say something mean. He's the worst bully in the school.

"That shows how much you know, Nick," I said. "That happens to be the one and only sock-picker-upper robot in the entire city."

He let out one of his hippo snort laughs, and with it came a blast of hot air that curled the hair on my neck.

"Please take your stinky breath off my neck," I said, "and pant somewhere else."

"People love my breath," McKelty panted.

"What planet do you live on?" I shot back.

We could have gone on forever, but Ms. Flowers was already telling us to stand to say the Pledge of Allegiance.

It seemed like forever until lunchtime. I couldn't concentrate on anything. Not the times tables. Not the spelling words. Not even the science chapter Ms. Flowers read to us about the three types of clouds. All I could think about was whether or not Jaden would help me finish Stanley. I couldn't wait to see if we could get him to pick up the socks.

When the lunch bell rang, Frankie, Ashley, and I were the first ones into the lunchroom. Kids were talking and laughing as they headed to their usual tables. We found Jaden sitting alone at a table in the corner, wearing his vest and tie. He was taking each baggie out of his lunch box and carefully arranging them all in front of him so nothing was touching anything else.

"Hey, buddy," I said as we walked over to him. "We've been looking for you."

He seemed surprised and then went back to arranging his baggies.

"So, Jaden," I said. "I really need your help. I have a major motor problem."

"Is your motor single or double output?" he asked.

"That's the problem. I don't know. I don't even know what any of those words mean. Could you translate, please?"

He didn't answer that, just looked back down at his lunch. It was the neatest lunch I had ever seen—one little sandwich that was a perfect square, one cookie, one graham cracker, a bag of grapes, and a box of apple juice.

"Great-looking lunch," Ashley said.

"Every day I have thirty-three grapes," Jaden explained.

"Wow, that's a lot of grapes," Frankie said. "My mom told me not to eat too many grapes at lunch or I'll spend the rest of the afternoon in the bathroom."

We all cracked up. Jaden didn't laugh. He just opened the baggie and started popping grapes into his mouth, so I thought I'd better get down to business. I took the motor out of my bag and unwrapped it. Then I brought Stanley out and put him on the lunch table in front of Jaden.

"We don't know how to connect the motor to make my robot's wheels and arms work," I began. "Can you just tell us how to attach it?"

"You'll need a four-channel drive

to get a multidirectional effect, of course," he said.

"Sure, that goes without saying," I said, nodding, even though I didn't have a clue what he was talking about.

"And since there are four joints, you'll need a Y-split servo cable," he went on.

Oh boy. This was so far over my head, a spaceship couldn't reach it.

"Do you think you could explain that a little more?" Frankie asked.

"It's really quite simple once you've seen it demonstrated," Jaden said, popping in another grape.

"I have a great idea," I said. "Why don't you come to my house after school today?"

"Why would I do that?" Jaden asked, looking up at me. It was the first time he actually looked me in the eye, and it was only for a second.

"You know, like a play date," I said.

He didn't answer.

"Look, Jaden," I went on. "I know it seems weird for me to ask for your help, because you're in the robot competition, too. But I don't know what else to do. My robot, Stanley, isn't nearly as cool as your husky robot. I just want him to work well enough so I can be part of the contest."

There was another silence.

"I don't have play dates," Jaden said at last.

"Hey, dude, there's a first time for everything," Frankie said.

"I'll tell my mom to make sure we have lots of grapes for you," I added.

"I've already had thirty-three," Jaden said. "That's my limit."

"Come on, Jaden," Ashley said. "It'll be fun. We don't bite."

But it seemed that Jaden wasn't listening anymore. He was

folding up his empty baggies and putting them neatly back in his lunch box.

"I have to go now," he said.

"So we'll see you later?" I asked hopefully.

He didn't answer, just got up and walked away.

"There goes my last hope," I said to Frankie and Ashley.

"Maybe not," Frankie said. "He didn't actually say no."

"He didn't say yes, either," I said.

I was trying to be positive, but deep down, I knew Jaden was never going to show up.

CHAPTER 7

Just as I thought, by four o'clock in the afternoon, Jaden still hadn't shown up at my house. Frankie, Ashley, and I sat around my dining-room table, our faces cupped in our hands, staring at poor half-done Stanley. My dad had played a video for us on how to install motors step-by-step. But after he took his computer into the kitchen to work, all of the steps slid out of our brains like melting ice cream.

"We tried as hard as we could," Frankie sighed, "but this motor stuff is just too hard for us."

"We're out of time," Ashley said. "But we shouldn't feel bad, we're only second-graders. I bet by the time we're in fourth grade, we'll be able to send a robot to the moon."

"There's always a chance that Jaden will still show up," I said. "Maybe he stopped to buy some grapes."

"Let's face it, Zip," Frankie said. "If he's not here by now, he's not coming."

Well, that wasn't exactly true, because no sooner had Frankie finished his sentence than the doorbell rang. All three of us jumped up like we were on a trampoline and bolted for the door. I flung it open, expecting to see Jaden.

But it wasn't. It was a woman with big curly hair who looked kind of familiar. I had seen her waiting outside after school, but I didn't know her name.

"Are you a friend of my mom's?" I blurted out.

"No, but I'd like to be. Are you Hank? I'm Jaden's mom."

I looked to see if Jaden was behind her, but the hallway was empty.

"So you came to say that Jaden couldn't make it?" I tried not to let my disappointment show, but I didn't do a very good job.

"Jaden," she said to no one. "Come and say hi. Hank really wants to see you."

I stepped out into the hall to see who she was talking to. Jaden was standing in the corner, next to Mrs. Fink's apartment. He was trying to hide, but he also didn't do a very good job.

"Jaden!" I screamed. "You

made it! Come on in! We've been waiting for you."

I turned and ran into the living room, then suddenly realized that Jaden wasn't behind me. I spun around and went back to the front door. Jaden hadn't moved.

"It takes Jaden some time to get comfortable in a new situation," his mom said softly.

"Oh, no problem," I said to Jaden. "I can fix that. I'll bring you my special pillow to sit on. It's so comfortable, it will make your butt smile."

Jaden just looked at me. Then, for the first time since I'd met him, he burst out laughing.

"That was funny," he said.

"If you think I'm funny, wait until you hear Frankie. He's hilarious. Come on in. We've got my robot all set up, but we don't know how to attach the motor."

That got Jaden's attention. Without another word, he took off and flew by me into our apartment.

"You can come, too," I said to his mom. "My dad's working in the kitchen. He's not that much fun to talk to, but at least he's a grown-up."

Jaden's mom laughed and gave me a little hug. She seemed really happy.

"Or you could go to my sister's room and visit with her and her pet iguana," I said, "but only if you like things that hiss—because they both do."

"I'll just pop my head into the kitchen to say hi to your father," she said. "Then, if you don't mind, I'll sit in the living room and read while you kids work on the robot. I always bring a book. Jaden likes to know I'm nearby."

After she came in, I raced to the dining room, where Jaden had already sat down in front of Stanley. He pulled out the same little screwdriver he had with him at school.

"Wow, Jaden, you sure came prepared," Ashley said.

Jaden didn't answer. He just took the motor and studied it, untangling the six colored wires that came out of it.

"We took that motor from an old front loader truck of mine," I explained.

"Excellent," he said. "Then it has lifting elements, or as you might call them, arms."

"Actually, we call them a plastic fork and a baby spoon," I said. It wasn't the funniest joke in the world, but it made me laugh. Jaden's face didn't change. He was in full-focus mode.

"How do you know what each

of those wires is for?" Frankie asked Jaden.

"Oh, that's simple," Jaden said without looking up. "The yellow wires go to the robot's lifting elements. The green wires attach to the back wheel electrical connection. The white wires attach to the connector that controls the front wheels, which seem to be made of toilet paper rolls. That's unusual."

"It was all we could find that was round and rolled," I explained. "And we wrapped them in Scotch tape to make them stronger."

He nodded and said, "Science is about solving problems."

Jaden didn't talk after that.

He got right to work, connecting the wires that went to each set of wheels. I watched him carefully.

"Hey, I'd like to try doing that," I said.

"Okay, then you attach the wires that go to the arms," Jaden said.

And I did.

Then I picked up the remote control to see if Stanley worked. And sure enough, he did!

When Stanley moved forward and backward, I was so happy, I thought my head was going to blow off. And when Stanley lifted his arms to scoop up a sock we had put in front of him, it felt like a miracle had happened right there on our dining-room table.

“Whoaaaaaa!” I yelled. “Stanley lives!”

Ashley, Frankie, and I high-fived until our palms hurt. We tried to high-five with Jaden, too, but he put his hands in his pockets. That was okay with me, though. Jaden had helped me make Stanley move, so he could do anything he wanted.

And what he wanted to do was leave.

"I'm going now," he said.

"Why don't you hang out with us for a while?" I asked. "We can have some crackers and peanut butter."

"I have to go," he said. "Mom!"

His mother stood up right away, but Jaden was already on his way to the front door.

"Thanks so much for including him, kids," she said. "You don't know how much Jaden and I appreciate your invitation."

"Maybe he can come back sometime and we'll build something else," I said.

"That's a great idea," Frankie chimed in.

"Mom!" Jaden called from the front door. "We have to go."

With a quick wave to us, she was off.

After she left, Frankie, Ashley, and I took turns with the remote control, moving Stanley all around the table and having him practice picking up socks. It was so much fun. I could hardly wait to show him off the next day at the school contest.

I continued playing with Stanley even after Ashley and Frankie had to go home for dinner. I was so proud of my little robot, I called my dad in to show him off.

"Look at this, Dad!" I said. "He goes backward and forward, and his arms go up and down like a forklift. I can hardly wait to show Mom."

"Your mother is working late," my dad said. "The Museum of Natural History is having an opening of the new dinosaur exhibit tonight, and the Crunchy Pickle is supplying all the sandwich platters."

"I didn't know dinosaurs liked salami sandwiches," I said.

My dad didn't hear my joke. He was staring at Stanley and rubbing his chin like he does when he looks over my homework and tells me I didn't do

the last row of math problems.

"Have you tried having your robot pick up an actual sock?" he asked. "That will be the real test."

"Check," I said. "Stanley can do it all."

"Do you feel like you really learned how to build this robot?" my dad asked.

"It's easy peasy, Dad," I said, with a little too much confidence. "Sit down, I'll show you."

It was really important to me to show my dad that I had learned how to do this. I removed each of the six wires.

"Now," I said, "all I have to do is use a screwdriver and put each wire back in its place."

I put the green wires on the back wheels, the yellow wires on the front wheels, and the white wires on Stanley's arms. All of a sudden, I had a feeling of panic. Was it green wires on the back, or did they go to the arms? And those yellow wires, did they go on the front wheels or the back? It was the same feeling I get just before a spelling test. I know the words. And then I don't.

I took a deep breath and picked up the remote control.

Just then, my dad's phone rang.

"Hello," he said. "Oh, Charlie. I'm glad you called."

He took the phone from his ear and whispered to me. "Hank, I have to take this. I might be a while. I'll see your robot at school tomorrow. Now get to your homework."

"No problem, Dad," I whispered back. "I'm just going to mess around with Stanley for a little while longer."

"Homework, now!" my dad said in a tone of voice you don't argue with. I took Stanley and put him into my mom's grocery bag along with the remote control.

"Get some rest, little guy," I whispered to him. "We have a big day tomorrow!"

CHAPTER 8

The competition was scheduled for after lunch in the multipurpose room. I was so nervous during lunch that I didn't even eat. That's only happened to me two other times in my whole life. Once was before I played in the big basketball championship game against PS 91. The other time was when the cafeteria was serving fish sticks that looked like they were still swimming on the plate.

After lunch, I walked down the hall to the multipurpose room. Frankie and Ashley were by my side. They never stopped encouraging me. And I never stopped thanking them.

"You guys were with me all the way," I said.

"Hey, that's what friends are for," Frankie said.

"Stanley's going to knock everyone's socks off," Ashley said.

"As a matter of fact, he already did," I answered, pointing to a girl in front of me who was wearing sneakers with no socks.

We were laughing so hard, I almost dropped Stanley.

"Be careful there," Frankie

said. "Stanley's big moment is coming up. You don't want him to fall apart before you get onstage."

When we walked into the multipurpose room, it was buzzing with excitement. All the kids in the school were there, except for the kindergartners, because those lucky little guys get to leave school early. All the parents that could come to watch the competition were there, and all the teachers, too. Leo, the school handyman, was sitting in the front row. Even the lunch ladies, with their hairnets still on, had shown up to watch.

Those of us who made robots got to sit up onstage in a semicircle around Principal Love. We each had our robots in our laps. Jaden was there holding his Alaskan husky robot that could bury bones. I wondered how he was going to demonstrate that, since the stage was made of wood. Then I noticed that he had a box of dirt at his feet. I should have known.

He's the kind of kid who thinks of everything.

Next to Jaden was Luke Whitman, whose robot looked like a hand with one long finger. Luke is a champion nose-picker. I had a creepy feeling that I knew what that long robot finger was for.

Next to Luke was a girl whose name was George Henry. She was all smiles. I would have been

grinning, too, if I had a cool robot like hers. It looked like a ballet dancer and even had a tutu made from sparkly tinsel that people put on Christmas trees.

There were four other kids. They all had one thing in common. They looked pretty serious. And so did their robots. One robot looked like a car, one was a space rocket, and one was a giant ant with moving jaws.

"Welcome to PS 87's first ever Build-a-Robot competition," Principal Love said into the microphone. "This is a day when we get to see how our young people have combined science with their imaginations."

Wow, I actually understood what Principal Love said. Usually, he goes on so long that I'm lost after "Welcome." I took that as a sign that good things were about to happen for Stanley and me.

"We have put the names of our contestants into a hat to see who goes first." Principal Love reached his hand into a PS 87 baseball cap and pulled out a slip of paper.

"George Henry," he called out. "George, come forward and show us your robot."

George took her ballerina and placed it on the floor in the center of the stage.

"Hello, everyone," she began. "My robot is named Raspberry Swirl, because I love ice cream. Her talent is spinning on her toes, but here's the special part. When she spins really fast, she turns a bowl filled with cream and sugar and chocolate syrup into chocolate ice cream."

I looked down at Stanley. Suddenly he seemed very plain. I wanted to cover his ears so he wouldn't feel bad, but then I remembered that he didn't have ears. So I covered mine instead.

When George turned the motor on, Raspberry Swirl started to spin so fast that all the tinsel on her skirt stuck straight out. The bowl spun really fast, too. When George hit the stop button, she showed everyone what was inside the bowl. It wasn't exactly ice cream. It was more like chocolate ice-cream soup. I think George Henry made up a brand-new dessert.

"Well done, George," Principal Love said as everyone clapped. "That looks extremely chocolate-y."

He reached into the hat and drew the next name. I was hoping it was me and also hoping it was not me, both at the same time. It wasn't me.

"Jaden W. is next," Principal Love said. "I'm sure he has something very interesting to show us."

I looked over at Jaden, but he didn't look back. He walked to the center of the stage, just staring down at the floor. I was hoping he would do really well.

But there was one major problem. Nick the Tick McKelty was sitting in the front row, with his big mouth attached to his big stupid head.

"I bet he made a weird robot," he said in a whisper loud enough for Jaden to hear.

"Mr. McKelty, keep your comments to yourself," Principal Love said.

A group of kids sitting near McKelty started to snicker. Jaden never even looked up at them. He just picked up his robot and ran off the stage to his mother, who was sitting in the audience. I saw her try to hug him, but he wouldn't let her.

I felt so bad for Jaden. I got up and walked over to Principal Love and whispered in his ear.

"Jaden worked really hard on his robot," I said. "Can you please give him another chance?"

Principal Love nodded.

"Jaden, would you like to try again?" he said into the microphone. "We would all love to see what you've created."

Jaden shook his head no. I wanted to go over to him and tell him not to pay any attention to that slime ball McKelty. But just as I stood up, Principal Love reached into the hat and called my name.

My heart raced as I walked to the center of the stage. My hand was shaking so hard that I could hear Stanley rattle inside the grocery bag. I looked around at all those people in the audience staring at me. I took a deep breath.

"All right, Stanley," I whispered. "It's showtime!"

CHAPTER 9

I took Stanley out of his grocery bag and held him up for all the audience to see.

"Ladies and gentlemen, boys and girls of all ages," I said. "I would like you to meet my robot, the super-duper sock-picker-upper. He's named Stanley, after my father."

I looked at my parents, who were sitting in the audience. I was so glad that my mom could get away from work. And my dad had such a proud smile on his face. I saw him give my mom a nudge with his elbow. She gave him a pat on the shoulder.

"How many people here are told every day to pick up their socks and put them in the hamper?" I asked, raising my own hand. Lots of other kids raised their hands, too. Even a few of the parents chuckled and raised their hands.

"We all know that picking up

socks is annoying," I said, "but I, Hank Zipzer, have the solution."

I reached in the bag and pulled out two socks. They didn't match, even though I was positive I had put a matching pair in there. I placed the socks on the floor as if nothing was wrong. Then I put one of our wooden salad bowls nearby.

"Watch and be amazed," I told the audience. "You will see Stanley pick up the socks and drop them in the salad bowl, which is playing the part of a hamper. Take a bow, Mr. Salad Bowl."

The audience laughed. *This is going well.*

Taking the remote control, I pressed the forward button and

waited for Stanley to roll across the stage to the socks. He did just the opposite. He rolled *away* from the socks, and when I say away, I mean *far away*.

Correction. This is not going so well.

"You can't tell forward from backward, Zipper Teeth," McKelty shouted. "Looks like your robot's got the same problem."

I looked down at the remote control. I had pressed the forward button. Why wasn't Stanley listening?

"Seems like my little robot has a mind of his own," I said to the audience. I was smiling on the outside, but shaking on the inside. "Let's try again, okay, Stanley?"

I pushed the forward button all the way down with my thumb. Stanley lurched backward again, this time at full speed. He was going so fast, he rolled right up onto Principal Love's sneakers and only stopped when his wheels got tangled up in Principal Love's shoelaces. You could hear Stanley's motor whirring, but he wasn't going anywhere.

Everyone was laughing at me, especially Nick McKelty.

"Nice move, loser," he called out.

I wasn't going to let him get away with that, so I said the first thing that came to my mind.

"Stanley," I said. "You're supposed to pick socks *up* off the floor, not pull them *off* Principal Love's feet!"

The audience laughed again, but this time they were laughing *with* me.

"Don't move, Principal Love," I said. "I've got this under control."

I went over to him, knelt down, and lifted Stanley off his sneakers. Well, I pulled most of him off. My sister's polka-dot spoon in the shape of a kitten stayed behind in the shoelaces. Poor Stanley was now officially missing an arm.

"Looks like your so-called robot is a total flop," McKelty called out.

"Mr. McKelty, if I have to remind you one more time, I will have to ask you to leave this assembly," Principal Love said. "We don't make fun of others here."

I just stood there holding Stanley. I was frozen. Stanley had worked so well on our dining-room table. I couldn't figure out what was going wrong. I knew I had to do something with all those eyeballs staring at me. But what?

Suddenly, from the corner of my eye, I saw Jaden rush up to the stage. He came up right next to me, and without saying a word, pulled out his little screwdriver. Taking Stanley from my hands, he sat down right there on the stage floor and started to rewire Stanley's motor.

Of course! That was the problem. When I rewired Stanley for my dad, I had gotten the wiring all wrong. No surprise there: My brain thinks it knows what it's doing, but most of the time, it gets confused.

"Green wires go to the back wheels, white wires to the front wheels, yellow wires to the arms," Jaden reminded me.

"This always happens to me," I whispered to him. "I get everything mixed up."

"You have to focus," Jaden said. "I'm really good at that. Here, you attach the last wire."

"Mr. Zipzer," Principal Love said. "Can we expect you to

continue anytime soon? Or should we move on?"

"Almost done, Principal Love," I said.

When I turned back around, I saw Jaden stand up and start to walk off the stage.

"Jaden, wait," I called out.

"You know what to do," Jaden said. "I've left you my screwdriver."

"Thanks a ton, Jaden," I whispered.

Then he left the stage and returned to his mom.

My hands were a little shaky as I picked up Jaden's screwdriver and attached the yellow wires to Stanley's arm. When I was finished, I turned to the audience and forced myself to put on a big smile.

"Stanley will now pick up a sock, and this time, using only one arm," I announced. "That's how good he is."

I held my breath and pushed the forward button on the remote control. This time, Stanley zipped forward, heading for the blue sock lying in the center of the stage. I stopped him right in front of the sock and pushed the yellow button that controlled his arms.

Stanley lowered his takeout-fork arm and scooped up the blue sock from the floor. I could hear the audience start to applaud.

"Now, Stanley," I called out, "I want you to drop the sock in the salad-bowl hamper!"

I pressed hard on the remote control button to lower Stanley's arm. I must have pressed it too hard, because suddenly, the remote control made a strange noise like popcorn popping. Then Stanley's arm shot up and flipped the sock high into the air.

The sock continued flying through the air, and landed—I'm sorry to say—right on Principal Love's nose. He looked like a puffin with an extra-long beak. Everyone in the whole room howled with laughter. Everyone but Principal Love. He just reached up with two fingers and carefully lifted my sock off his face like it was a wet noodle.

Standing there on the stage, I had three thoughts at the exact same time.

My first thought was that Jaden really came through for me, like a true friend does.

My second thought was how happy I was that I picked clean socks so that Principal Love didn't have to smell my dirty ones.

My third thought was that I probably was not going to win this contest.

CHAPTER 10

I watched the rest of the competition from my chair on the stage. It was amazing. You never know how smart and creative the kids around you are until they have a chance to show it off.

Take Ryan Shimozato. He put a model rocket engine into his spaceship robot, and it flew all the way to the first row of chairs, where his brother Bobby caught it in a butterfly net. And Gracie Maloof's giant ant robot actually chewed on a large green leaf of kale just like a real leaf-cutter ant would do. And then she made it burp.

Luke Whitman's robot was classic Luke Whitman. He pushed a button, and the long finger on his robot hand started to turn. Then he held the finger up to his face, and yes, put it right into his nose. I will not describe what happened next, no matter how much you ask. Trust me, I am helping you not throw up.

Principal Love ended Luke's demonstration early.

"Thank you for your participation, Mr. Whitman," he said. "I think we've all seen more than enough."

"But I haven't even gotten to the snot yet," Luke answered.

"My point exactly." Principal Love led Luke to his seat. "Please sit down," he said. "And here's my personal handkerchief. Do not worry about giving it back."

When all of us had demonstrated our robots, Principal Love called two of the teachers up onstage to help him pick the winner.

While they were talking, everyone had to listen to Artie Higgenbottom play "This Land Is Your Land" on his viola. I could see most of the kids in the audience putting their fingers in their ears to block out the sound.

Finally, the two teachers and Principal Love reached a decision. I felt excited as Principal Love came to the center of the stage. Even though part of me knew I didn't have much chance to win, the other part of me had its fingers crossed. As my dad always says, "It's not over until it's over."

"We have chosen a winner," Principal Love announced. "For her combination of creativity and scientific thinking, first place goes to George Henry and her ice-cream-making ballerina robot, Raspberry Swirl."

George Henry was so excited that she jumped up and twirled all the way from her chair to Principal

Love. He handed her the trophy, which she kissed and then held up over her head for everyone to see.

To be totally honest, I was a little disappointed that I didn't win that big, shiny trophy. Okay, that was only kind of honest. I was very disappointed. I could just see that trophy sitting on my desk, right next to my jar of colored pencils. But as I watched George Henry twirl into the audience to hug her parents, I thought, *Good for her.*

When the audience's applause for George Henry had died down, Principal Love gave out the rest of the awards. Ryan's rocket got second place, and Gracie's leaf-cutter ant took third.

Too bad, Hank, I thought to myself. *Looks like you didn't win anything.*

But then a great thing happened.

"To reward all the students who participated in our Build-a-Robot competition," Principal Love said, "each of you will receive an honorable mention certificate with the PS 87 gold seal."

Wow! My ears almost jumped off my head. A certificate with a gold seal! I'd never gotten one of those before. I leaped out of my chair and marched right up to Principal Love.

"I'd like to say a few words," I said.

"A very few, Mr. Zipzer," Principal Love whispered. "This is highly unusual."

I took the microphone.

"This is my first honorable mention ever," I said. "And it wouldn't have happened without the help of my friends, Ashley, Frankie, and Jaden. And especially Jaden, who is a genius at robots, and who really comes through when you need him."

I could see Ashley and Frankie high-fiving each other. Jaden sat quietly next to his mom. I gave him my best Zipzer wave. I couldn't believe my eyes when I saw him wave back.

When the assembly ended, I ran into the crowd to show my mom and dad my certificate. On the way, I bumped smack into Nick McKelty. It's hard not to bump into him because his mouth alone takes up so much room.

"Stop flapping that stupid piece of paper around," he said to me. "It looks like you're trying to fly."

"This happens to be an honorable mention certificate," I said. "With a gold seal on it."

"Boy, are you a dork," McKelty said. "Didn't you notice that everyone in the competition got one?"

"Actually, what I did notice is that you didn't get one," I said.

As I walked away and left him there with his big mouth hanging open, I felt great. Putting him in his place was as good as winning.

My mom and dad were so proud of me that they suggested we all go to Harvey's to celebrate with pizza.

"It's only two blocks away,"

my dad said. "And besides, I have a coupon for two dollars off that they sent in the mail."

"Maybe Ashley and Frankie want to join us," my mom suggested. "I can call their parents."

I didn't even have to ask Frankie and Ashley if they wanted to come. You say pizza, and they're there.

As we headed for the door, I saw Jaden walking out with his mom.

"Would it be okay if we asked Jaden and his mom to come along, too?" I asked my parents. "Dad, you did say you had a coupon."

"He'll probably say no," Frankie said.

"Ask him anyway, Hank," my mom said. "Let it be his choice."

I walked up to Jaden and said, "Hey, we're all going for pizza at Harvey's. Do you want to come?"

Jaden looked at me for what seemed like a long time.

"I only eat pizza with grapes," he said at last.

"That could be a problem," I said. "Harvey's has pepperoni pizza, and mushroom pizza, and even pineapple pizza. But I'm pretty sure they don't have grape pizza."

Jaden reached into his pocket and pulled out a plastic baggie filled with his usual bunch of grapes.

"I always carry my own," he said.

"Well, come on then," I said. "One grape pizza, coming right up."

"You don't have to invite me," Jaden said.

"But I want to," I told him.

So we all went to Harvey's and sat around a big table. Ashley, Frankie, and I insisted that Jaden put his husky dog robot in the middle of the table and give us our own demonstration. We all cheered when it dug out a big clump of parmesan cheese from the bowl on the table.

When our pizza arrived, Jaden made his robot dump the parmesan cheese onto the pizza and put the first slice on my plate. That was pretty cool!

"Your son is very talented," my mom said to Jaden's mom.

"I've always known that to be true," his mom said. "Thank you for noticing."

I held up my slice of pizza and made a toast.

"Here's to Ashley, Frankie, and Jaden," I said. "Otherwise known as Team Stanley."

Jaden looked surprised.

"I've never been part of a team before," he said.

"You are now," I said. Ashley, Frankie, and I brought our pizza slices together, cheered, and then took that first great bite.

Jaden reached into his baggie, pulled out a grape, and put it right on the end of his slice. Then he took a bite.

I saw Jaden break into a big smile.

And the rest of us did, too.

CHAPTER 11
THREE THINGS I LEARNED FROM BUILDING STANLEY THE ROBOT
BY HANK ZIPZER
1. It's good to try new things, even if they seem hard for you.
2. Those kids in your school that no one ever talks to, you should give them a chance. They could be really cool.
3. Grapes on pizza are pretty tasty.